Authentic Christianity: The Heart of Old Time Religion

Joshua Rhoades

Published by Joshua Paul Rhoades, 2024.

This is a work of fiction. Similarities to real people, places, or events are entirely coincidental.

AUTHENTIC CHRISTIANITY: THE HEART OF OLD TIME RELIGION

First edition. August 22, 2024.

Copyright © 2024 Joshua Rhoades.

ISBN: 979-8227680594

Written by Joshua Rhoades.

Also by Joshua Rhoades

Courage Under Fire: David's Stand On The Battlefield
Jonah's Journey: Voices Of Redemption And Lessons In Obedience
The Furnace Of Faith: 12 Principles From The Heat Of Faith
Whispers of Hope: Inspiring Stories of Men's Prayers In Scripture
Frontier Legends: The Oregon Dream
Elijah: A Beacon Of Boldness
HOOK, LINE & SAVIOUR - Faith Reflections from Fishing
Driven By Faith: Motor Racing Inspired Christian Life
30 Day Devotional - Bold and Strong- Coffee Devotions for a
Courageous Christian Walk
Authentic Christianity: The Heart of Old Time Religion
Flee Fornication: The Plea For Purity
Renewed Hope- How to Find Encouragement in God
Sounding The Call - The Voice of Conviction
The Altar - Where Heaven Meets Earth
The Sacred Art of Silence - How Silence Speaks in Scripture

Chapter 1 – Divine and Perfect Bible

Authentic Christianity, the heart of old-time religion, is deeply rooted in the belief that the Bible is inspired, perfect, and preserved by God. This belief is essential because it means that the Bible is not just a book but the living Word of God, a guide for our lives, the source of truth, and the foundation for our faith. The unwavering conviction that God has provided an inspired, perfect, and preserved Bible is at the core of old-time religion. Scriptures such as 2 Timothy 3:16-17 affirm this: "All scripture is given by inspiration of God, and is profitable for doctrine, for reproof, for correction, for instruction in righteousness: That the man of God may be perfect, thoroughly furnished unto all good works." This verse tells us that every part of the Bible is inspired by God and helpful in teaching us what is true, making us realize what is wrong in our lives, correcting us when we are bad, and teaching us to do what is right. It equips us to do every good work God wants us to do. The Bible is the ultimate authority in all matters of faith and practice, a guide that has been divinely protected through the ages.

In the old-time religion, the Bible's role is central. It is God's inspired Word, meaning that God Himself breathed out every word in it. This belief is supported by passages like 2 Peter 1:21, which says, "For the prophecy came not in old time by the will of man: but holy men of God spake as they were moved by the Holy Ghost." This means that the Bible was not written by human will but by men guided by the Holy Spirit. This divine inspiration ensures that the Bible is perfect and without error. Proverbs 30:5 says, "Every word of God is pure: he is a shield unto them that put their trust in him." This purity and perfection mean that we can trust the Bible altogether.

The preservation of the Bible is also a critical belief in old-time religion. Despite the many attempts throughout history to destroy or discredit the Bible, it has remained intact and unchanged. Psalm 12:6-7 declares, "The words of the LORD are pure words: as silver tried in a furnace of earth, purified seven times. Thou shalt keep them, O LORD, thou shalt preserve them from this generation for ever." This promise of preservation means that God's Word will endure forever, unchanged and unbroken.

Because the Bible is inspired, perfect, and preserved, it is the ultimate authority in all matters of faith and practice. Isaiah 40:8 says, "The grass withereth, the flower fadeth: but the word of our God shall stand for ever." This verse reminds us that while everything else changes and fades, God's Word remains constant and eternal. This eternal nature of the Bible means that it is always relevant and applicable to our lives, no matter how much the world changes.

The Bible is also a guide for our lives. Psalm 119:105 tells us, "Thy word is a lamp unto my feet, and a light unto my path." This means that the Bible illuminates our path, showing us how we should go and help us avoid the pitfalls and dangers along the way. It provides wisdom and direction for every situation we face. James 1:5 encourages us to seek wisdom from God, saying, "If any of you lack wisdom, let him ask of God, that giveth to all men liberally, and upbraideth not; and it shall be given him." The Bible is one of God's primary ways to give us this wisdom.

The Bible is also the source of truth. John 17:17 says, "Sanctify them through thy truth: thy word is truth." This means the Bible is the standard by which all other truth is measured. In a world where many claim to have the truth, the Bible is the ultimate authority, the final word on what is true and what is not. It teaches us about God's character, will, and life plan. It reveals to us who we are, why we are here, and what our purpose is.

In addition to being the guide and the source of truth, the Bible is also the foundation for our faith. Romans 10:17 says, "So then faith cometh by hearing, and hearing by the word of God." This means that our faith is built on the Word of God. The more we read and study the Bible, the more our faith strengthens. It provides the solid ground upon which we can stand, giving us confidence and assurance in our relationship with God.

Because the Bible is inspired, perfect, and preserved, it is not just a book to be read but a book to be lived. James 1:22 says, "But be ye doers of the word, and not hearers only, deceiving your own selves." This means that we are to practice what we read in the Bible. It should shape our thoughts, our words, and our actions. It should influence every aspect of our lives, from how we treat others to how we make decisions and spend our time.

In the old-time religion, the Bible is not just a source of knowledge but a transformation. Hebrews 4:12 says, "For the word of God is quick, and powerful, and sharper than any twoedged sword, piercing even to the dividing asunder of soul and spirit, and of the joints and marrow, and is a discerner of the thoughts and intents of the heart." This means that the Bible can change us from the inside out. It reveals our innermost thoughts and desires, convicting us of sin and leading us to repentance. It helps us to grow in righteousness and holiness, becoming more like Christ.

The Bible is also the source of comfort and encouragement. Romans 15:4 says, "For whatsoever things were written aforetime were written for our learning, that we through patience and comfort of the scriptures might have hope." This means that the Bible provides hope and encouragement for us in times of trouble. It reminds us of God's faithfulness and His promises. It assures us that God is with us and will see us through no matter what we are going through.

The Bible also plays a crucial role in the church. It is the basis for preaching and teaching, as 2 Timothy 4:2 says, "Preach the word; be instant in season, out of season; reprove, rebuke, exhort with all longsuffering and doctrine." This means that the Bible should be central to all the church does. It is the standard by which all doctrine and practice are measured. It is the source of instruction and guidance for the church, helping it to stay true to its mission and purpose.

In summary, authentic Christianity, the heart of old-time religion, is grounded in the belief that God inspired, perfected, and preserved the Bible. This belief is essential because it means that the Bible is not just a book but the living Word of God, the guide for our lives, the source of truth, and the foundation for our faith. It equips us to do every good work God wants, provides wisdom and direction for every situation, and reveals who we are, why we are here, and our purpose. It is not just a source of knowledge but the source of transformation, changing us from the inside out. It is the source of comfort and encouragement, providing hope in times of trouble. It plays a crucial role in the church, serving as the basis for preaching and teaching. As we hold fast to the inspired, perfect, and preserved Bible, we can navigate life's challenges with confidence and assurance, knowing that we are standing on the solid ground of God's Word. This is the heart of old-time religion, the foundation of authentic Christianity.

Chapter 2 - Direction of the Spirit of God

Authentic Christianity, the heart of old-time religion, emphasizes following the leading of the Spirit of God. This is a central aspect because it means living a life guided and directed by the Holy Spirit in every aspect. Romans 8:14 states, "For as many as are led by the Spirit of God, they are the sons of God." This verse highlights the importance of sensitivity to the Spirit's leading, showing that those who follow the Holy Spirit are indeed children of God. Being led by the Holy Spirit involves seeking His wisdom and direction in all decisions relying on Him for guidance and understanding.

The Holy Spirit is our guide, comforter, and teacher. John 14:26 says, "But the Comforter, which is the Holy Ghost, whom the Father will send in my name, he shall teach you all things, and bring all things to your remembrance, whatsoever I have said unto you." This means that the Holy Spirit teaches us everything we need to know and helps us remember the teachings of Jesus. A life led by the Spirit is constantly learning and growing in the knowledge of God.

In old-time religion, believers are encouraged to live in the Spirit and walk in the Spirit. Galatians 5:16 says, "This I say then, Walk in the Spirit, and ye shall not fulfil the lust of the flesh." Walking in the Spirit means living according to the Spirit's guidance and not following our sinful desires. It means allowing the Holy Spirit to influence our thoughts, actions, and decisions, helping us to live a life that pleases God.

The presence of the Holy Spirit in our lives is a sign that we belong to God. Ephesians 1:13-14 says, "In whom ye also trusted, after that ye heard the word of truth, the gospel of your salvation: in whom also after that ye believed, ye were sealed with that holy Spirit of promise, Which is the earnest of our inheritance until the redemption of the purchased possession, unto the praise of his glory." This passage tells us that the Holy Spirit seals God's ownership and guarantees our inheritance in

Christ. The Holy Spirit assures us of our salvation and reminds us that we are children of God.

Being led by the Spirit also involves producing the fruit of the Spirit in our lives. Galatians 5:22-23 lists these fruits: "But the fruit of the Spirit is love, joy, peace, longsuffering, gentleness, goodness, faith, Meekness, temperance: against such there is no law." When we follow the leading of the Holy Spirit, these qualities become evident in our lives. They are the visible evidence of the Holy Spirit's work within us, showing that we live following God's will.

In addition to guiding us, the Holy Spirit helps us with our weaknesses and intercedes with us in prayer. Romans 8:26-27 says, "Likewise the Spirit also helpeth our infirmities: for we know not what we should pray for as we ought: but the Spirit itself maketh intercession for us with groanings which cannot be uttered. And he that searcheth the hearts knoweth what is the mind of the Spirit, because he maketh intercession for the saints according to the will of God." This means that even when we do not know what to pray for, the Holy Spirit prays for us according to God's will, helping us in our times of need.

The Holy Spirit also empowers us to serve and be witnesses. Acts 1:8 tells us, "But ye shall receive power, after that the Holy Ghost is come upon you: and ye shall be witnesses unto me both in Jerusalem, and in all Judaea, and in Samaria, and unto the uttermost part of the earth." This means that the Holy Spirit gives us the power to be effective witnesses for Christ, enabling us to share the gospel with boldness and conviction.

Living by the Spirit involves a daily surrender to His leading and an openness to His direction. Proverbs 3:5-6 advises, "Trust in the LORD with all thine heart; and lean not unto thine own understanding. In all thy ways acknowledge him, and he shall direct thy paths." This means we are to trust God completely, not relying on our understanding but acknowledging Him in all our ways and allowing Him to direct our paths. When we follow the leading of the Holy Spirit, we can be confident that He will guide us in the right direction.

The Holy Spirit also brings unity among believers. Ephesians 4:3-4 says, "Endeavouring to keep the unity of the Spirit in the bond of peace. There is one body, and one Spirit, even as ye are called in one hope of your calling." This means that the Holy Spirit unites us as one body in Christ, helping us to maintain peace and unity within the church. Following the leading of the Holy Spirit involves working towards unity and harmony with our fellow believers.

The Holy Spirit also convicts us of sin and leads us to repentance. John 16:8 says, "And when he is come, he will reprove the world of sin, and of righteousness, and of judgment." This means that the Holy Spirit convicts us of our sins, showing us where we have gone wrong and leading us to repentance. Following the leading of the Holy Spirit involves being sensitive to His conviction and responding with repentance and a desire to live a righteous life.

Being led by the Spirit also means living in freedom. 2 Corinthians 3:17 says, "Now the Lord is that Spirit: and where the Spirit of the Lord is, there is liberty." This means that the Holy Spirit brings freedom from the bondage of sin and the law, allowing us to live in the liberty of God's grace.

In the old-time religion, believers are encouraged to seek the filling of the Holy Spirit. Ephesians 5:18 says, "And be not drunk with wine, wherein is excess; but be filled with the Spirit." This means that we are to continually seek to be filled with the Holy Spirit, allowing Him to control and influence every area of our lives. Being filled with the Spirit empowers us to live a life that is pleasing to God and effective in His service.

The Holy Spirit also gives us spiritual gifts to build the church. 1 Corinthians 12:4-7 says, "Now there are diversities of gifts, but the same Spirit. And there are differences of administrations, but the same Lord. And there are diversities of operations, but it is the same God which worketh all in all. But the manifestation of the Spirit is given to every man to profit withal." This means that the Holy Spirit gives each believer different gifts for the common good. Following the leading of the Holy Spirit involves using these gifts to serve others and build up the church.

Living by the Spirit also means being transformed into the image of Christ. 2 Corinthians 3:18 says, "But we all, with open face beholding as in a glass the glory of the Lord, are changed into the same image from glory to glory, even as by the Spirit of the Lord." This means that as we follow the leading of the Holy Spirit, we are gradually transformed to become more like Christ. This transformation is a continual process, taking us from one degree of glory to another.

The Holy Spirit also helps us to understand and apply God's Word. John 16:13 says, "Howbeit when he, the Spirit of truth, is come, he will guide you into all truth: for he shall not speak of himself; but whatsoever he shall hear, that shall he speak: and he will shew you things to come." This means that the Holy Spirit guides us into all truth, helping us to understand and apply the teachings of the Bible. Following the leading of the Holy Spirit involves being attentive to His guidance as we read and study God's Word.

The Holy Spirit also produces spiritual fruit in our lives. Galatians 5:22-23 lists these fruits: "But the fruit of the Spirit is love, joy, peace, longsuffering, gentleness, goodness, faith, Meekness, temperance: against such there is no law." When we follow the leading of the Holy Spirit, these qualities become evident in our lives. They are the visible evidence of the Holy Spirit's work within us, showing that we live following God's will.

In summary, authentic Christianity, the heart of old-time religion, emphasizes following the leading of the Spirit of God. This involves being sensitive to the Spirit's guidance in every aspect of life, seeking His wisdom and direction in all decisions, and allowing Him to influence our thoughts, actions, and decisions. It means being taught and reminded of Jesus' teachings, living in the Spirit and walking in the Spirit, and producing the fruit of the Spirit in our lives. It involves being helped in our weaknesses, empowered for service and witness, and living in unity with other believers. It means being convicted of sin and led to repentance, living in freedom, seeking the filling of the Spirit, using our spiritual gifts for the common good, being transformed into the image of Christ, and understanding and applying God's Word. Following the leading of the Holy Spirit is essential for living a life that pleases God and fulfills His purposes. This is the heart of old-time religion, the foundation of authentic Christianity.

Chapter 3 -Devoting Singing Of The Godly

Authentic Christianity, the heart of old-time religion, emphasizes vocal grateful singing in a God-honoring fashion, a hallmark of our faith. This form of worship is deeply rooted in the Bible and is a vital expression of our love and gratitude to God. Colossians 3:16 encourages, "Let the word of Christ dwell in you richly in all wisdom; teaching and admonishing one another in psalms and hymns and spiritual songs, singing with grace in your hearts to the Lord." This verse highlights the importance of letting the message of Christ fill our lives, teaching and helping one another with all wisdom, and expressing our gratitude and reverence through song.

Singing hymns and spiritual songs with gratitude and reverence is not just about musical expression but about heartfelt adoration and thankfulness to God. In Ephesians 5:19, we are instructed, "Speaking to yourselves in psalms and hymns and spiritual songs, singing and making melody in your heart to the Lord." This verse shows that singing is a way to communicate with ourselves and others about God's goodness and greatness. It is a way to remind ourselves of His love, grace, and mercy and to express our joy and thankfulness.

The book of Psalms is filled with examples of vocal grateful singing. Psalm 95:1-2 says, "O come, let us sing unto the LORD: let us make a joyful noise to the rock of our salvation. Let us come before his presence with thanksgiving, and make a joyful noise unto him with psalms." These verses invite us to come before God with joyful songs and thanksgiving, recognizing Him as our Savior and the source of our joy. Psalm 100:1-2 echoes this call: "Make a joyful noise unto the LORD, all ye lands. Serve the LORD with gladness: come before his presence with singing." This shows that singing is a joyful and glad expression of our service and worship to God.

Singing gracefully to the Lord means our songs should be filled with gratitude and reverence. Hebrews 13:15 reminds us, "By him therefore let us offer the sacrifice of praise to God continually, that is, the fruit of our lips giving thanks to his name." This verse teaches us that our singing is a form of sacrifice, a way to praise God continually and thank His name. It is an act of worship that should be done with sincerity and a heart full of gratitude.

The apostle Paul and Silas demonstrated the power of singing hymns in Acts 16:25: "And at midnight Paul and Silas prayed, and sang praises unto God: and the prisoners heard them." Despite their suffering, they praised God, showing their deep faith and trust in Him. Their singing uplifted their spirits and served as a powerful witness to those around them.

Singing with a grateful heart is also a way to remember and declare God's mighty works. Psalm 105:2 says, "Sing unto him, sing psalms unto him: talk ye of all his wondrous works." This verse encourages us to sing about God's marvelous deeds, proclaiming His greatness and goodness. It is a way to keep His mighty works alive in our memories and to share them with others.

In old-time religion, singing is an activity that brings believers together in worship and unity. Psalm 133:1 states, "Behold, how good and how pleasant it is for brethren to dwell together in unity!" Singing together helps to foster this unity, as it is a shared expression of our faith and love for God. It is a way to join our voices and hearts in a common purpose, glorifying God and edifying one another.

The content of our songs is also essential. Colossians 3:16 emphasizes the use of psalms, hymns, and spiritual songs. Psalms are songs that come directly from the Scriptures, particularly the book of Psalms. Hymns are songs of praise written to honor and glorify God. Spiritual songs express our personal experiences and reflections on our relationship with God. All three types of songs are valuable and serve to enrich our worship.

Singing gracefully to the Lord means our songs should reflect our genuine love and devotion to God. Psalm 96:1-2 says, "O sing unto the LORD a new song: sing unto the LORD, all the earth. Sing unto the LORD, bless his name; shew forth his salvation from day to day." This verse encourages us to sing new songs to the Lord, blessing His name and proclaiming His salvation. Our singing should reflect our ongoing relationship with God and our desire to praise Him.

Singing also has a powerful impact on our hearts and minds. Psalm 147:1 declares, "Praise ye the LORD: for it is good to sing praises unto our God; for it is pleasant; and praise is comely." Singing praises to God is reasonable and pleasant but also fitting and appropriate. It helps to lift our spirits, bring joy to our hearts, and align our thoughts with God's truth.

Singing with gratitude and reverence also involves recognizing the greatness and majesty of God. Psalm 145:1-2 says, "I will extol thee, my God, O king; and I will bless thy name for ever and ever. Every day will I bless thee; and I will praise thy name for ever and ever." This verse shows the importance of daily praise and adoration, acknowledging God's greatness, and committing to praise Him continually.

Singing can provide comfort and strength in times of difficulty and trial. Psalm 42:8 says, "Yet the LORD will command his lovingkindness in the daytime, and in the night his song shall be with me, and my prayer unto the God of my life." This verse reminds us that God's song is with us even in the darkest times, providing us with hope and encouragement. Singing helps to remind us of God's presence and promises, giving us the strength to persevere.

Singing with a grateful heart also means recognizing God's goodness and faithfulness. Lamentations 3:22-23 says, "It is of the LORD's mercies that we are not consumed, because his compassions fail not. They are new every morning: great is thy faithfulness." This passage highlights God's unfailing mercy and faithfulness, which should inspire us to sing

His praises daily. Our songs should reflect our gratitude for His constant love and care.

In the context of old-time religion, singing is also a way to teach and reinforce biblical truths. Deuteronomy 31:19 instructs, "Now therefore write ye this song for you, and teach it the children of Israel: put it in their mouths, that this song may be a witness for me against the children of Israel." This verse shows that songs can be a powerful teaching tool, helping to instill God's truths in our hearts and minds. We reinforce our understanding of God's Word and His character by singing hymns and spiritual songs.

Singing with gratitude and reverence also involves a response to God's goodness. Psalm 98:1-2 says, "O sing unto the LORD a new song; for he hath done marvellous things: his right hand, and his holy arm, hath gotten him the victory. The LORD hath made known his salvation: his righteousness hath he openly shewed in the sight of the heathen." This passage highlights the importance of singing in response to God's marvelous deeds and His salvation. Our songs should be a response of praise and thanksgiving for all God has done.

The New Testament also encourages singing as a vital part of Christian worship. James 5:13 says, "Is any among you afflicted? let him pray. Is any merry? let him sing psalms." This verse shows that singing is an appropriate response to joy and a way to express our gladness. It is a natural outflow of a heart filled with the Lord's joy.

Singing gracefully to the Lord also involves a commitment to worshiping Him in spirit and truth. John 4:24 says, "God is a Spirit: and they that worship him must worship him in spirit and in truth." This means that our singing should be sincere and genuine, coming from a heart that truly seeks to honor God. It is not just about the outward act of singing but the inward attitude of reverence and devotion.

In summary, authentic Christianity, the heart of old-time religion, greatly emphasizes vocal grateful singing in a God-honoring fashion. This form of worship is deeply rooted in the Bible and is a vital expression of our love and gratitude to God. Singing hymns and spiritual songs with gratitude and reverence is not just about musical expression but about heartfelt adoration and thankfulness to God. It involves letting the word of Christ dwell in us richly, teaching and admonishing one another, and expressing our gratitude through song. It is a joyful and glad expression of our service and worship to God, a way to remember and declare His mighty works and foster unity among believers. Our songs should be filled with gratitude and reverence, reflecting our genuine love and devotion to God. Singing gracefully to the Lord helps lift our spirits, bring joy, and align our thoughts with God's truth. It is a response to God's goodness and faithfulness, a way to teach and reinforce biblical truths, and a commitment to worshiping Him in spirit and truth. As we sing with grateful hearts, we fulfill the biblical command to continually offer the sacrifice of praise to God, giving thanks to His name and glorifying Him in all that we do. This is the heart of old-time religion, the foundation of authentic Christianity.

Chapter 4 - Declaring the Good News

Authentic Christianity, the heart of old-time religion, emphasizes the vital mission of taking the Good News to everyone worldwide. Evangelism is a fundamental component of this faith, driven by the Great Commission found in Matthew 28:19-20, which commands, "Go ye therefore, and teach all nations, baptizing them in the name of the Father, and of the Son, and of the Holy Ghost: Teaching them to observe all things whatsoever I have commanded you." This directive from Jesus Himself underlines the importance of spreading the Gospel locally and globally, ensuring everyone can hear about Jesus Christ and His saving grace.

The mandate to share the Gospel is not limited by geography or cultural boundaries. Mark 16:15 further emphasizes this call, saying, "And he said unto them, Go ye into all the world, and preach the gospel to every creature." This means that the message of Jesus is intended for every person, regardless of their background or location. The universality of the Gospel message is central to old-time religion, reflecting the belief that all people need salvation through Jesus Christ.

A sense of urgency and compassion fuels evangelism. Romans 10:13-14 underscores the necessity of sharing the Good News, stating, "For whosoever shall call upon the name of the Lord shall be saved. How then shall they call on him in whom they have not believed? and how shall they believe in him of whom they have not heard? and how shall they hear without a preacher?" This passage highlights the critical role of believers in making sure that others hear the Gospel. Without someone to share the message, many would remain unaware of the salvation available through Jesus Christ.

The process of evangelism involves not only preaching but also teaching and discipling new believers. Matthew 28:20 instructs us to teach new disciples to "observe all things whatsoever I have commanded you." This means evangelism is about making converts and helping people grow in their faith and understanding God's Word. Acts 1:8 emphasizes the empowerment believers receive for this task: "But ye shall receive power, after that the Holy Ghost is come upon you: and ye shall be witnesses unto me both in Jerusalem, and in all Judaea, and in Samaria, and unto the uttermost part of the earth." The Holy Spirit equips and empowers believers to be effective witnesses for Christ.

The early church example in the Book of Acts is a powerful model for evangelism. Acts 2:41-42 describes how new believers were witnesses to the community: "Then they that gladly received his word were baptized: and the same day there were added unto them about three thousand souls. And they continued stedfastly in the apostles' doctrine and fellowship, and in breaking of bread, and in prayers." This demonstrates the importance of preaching the Gospel, baptizing new believers, and incorporating them into the church's life so that they can grow and be nurtured in their faith.

Evangelism is also an expression of love and obedience to Christ's command. John 14:15 says, "If ye love me, keep my commandments." One of the most precise ways to show our love for Jesus is by obeying His command to share the Gospel. This love for Christ compels us to reach out to others, sharing with them the hope and salvation we have found in Him. 2 Corinthians 5:14-15 explains this motivation: "For the love of Christ constraineth us; because we thus judge, that if one died for all, then were all dead: And that he died for all, that they which live should not henceforth live unto themselves, but unto him which died for them, and rose again." Our love for Christ and our recognition of His sacrifice drive us to share His message with others.

Evangelism is also rooted in our compassion for those who are lost. Matthew 9:36 shows Jesus' heart for the lost: "But when he saw the multitudes, he was moved with compassion on them, because they fainted, and were scattered abroad, as sheep having no shepherd." This compassion should inspire us to reach out to those spiritually lost and in need of the Good Shepherd. Jude 1:22-23 encourages us to act on this compassion: "And of some have compassion, making a difference: And others save with fear, pulling them out of the fire; hating even the garment spotted by the flesh." Our compassion can make a significant difference in the lives of those we reach with the Gospel.

The message we share is one of hope and salvation. John 3:16, one of the most well-known verses in the Bible, encapsulates this message: "For God so loved the world, that he gave his only begotten Son, that whosoever believeth in him should not perish, but have everlasting life." This message of God's love and the promise of eternal life through faith in Jesus Christ is at the heart of evangelism. Romans 6:23 further explains the need for this message: "For the wages of sin is death; but the gift of God is eternal life through Jesus Christ our Lord." The reality of sin and its consequences make the message of salvation all the more urgent and necessary.

Evangelism also involves a clear proclamation of the Gospel. 1 Corinthians 15:3-4 provides a concise summary of this message: "For I delivered unto you first of all that which I also received, how that Christ died for our sins according to the scriptures; And that he was buried, and that he rose again the third day according to the scriptures." This simple yet profound truth is the foundation of our faith and the message we are called to share with the world.

In addition to preaching and teaching, our lives testify to the Gospel's transforming power. Matthew 5:16 encourages us, "Let your light so shine before men, that they may see your good works, and glorify your Father which is in heaven." Our actions and how we live our lives can be a powerful witness to others, tangibly demonstrating the love and grace of God. Philippians 2:15-16 urges us to live blamelessly and shine as lights in the world: "That ye may be blameless and harmless, the sons of God, without rebuke, in the midst of a crooked and perverse nation, among whom ye shine as lights in the world; Holding forth the word of life." Our lives should reflect the Gospel we proclaim, serving as a beacon of hope to those around us.

Evangelism is also a collective effort involving the entire body of Christ. 1 Corinthians 3:6-9 highlights the collaborative nature of this work: "I have planted, Apollos watered; but God gave the increase. So then neither is he that planteth any thing, neither he that watereth; but God that giveth the increase. Now he that planteth and he that watereth are one: and every man shall receive his own reward according to his own labour. For we are labourers together with God: ye are God's husbandry, ye are God's building." This passage reminds us that while we each have different roles in evangelism, God ultimately brings about growth and transformation. "We must work together, supporting and encouraging one another in this vital mission."

The Great Commission is a continuous call, not limited to a one-time effort but an ongoing commitment. Acts 5:42 illustrates the early church's dedication to this mission: "And daily in the temple, and in every house, they ceased not to teach and preach Jesus Christ." This example challenges us to make evangelism a regular part of our lives, continually seeking opportunities to share the Gospel with those around us.

In the context of old-time religion, taking the Good News to everyone involves a deep sense of responsibility and privilege. 2 Corinthians 5:20 describes this role as being ambassadors for Christ: "Now then we are ambassadors for Christ, as though God did beseech you by us: we pray you in Christ's stead, be ye reconciled to God." As ambassadors, we represent Christ to the world, carrying His message of reconciliation and hope. This role requires us to be faithful, diligent, and compassionate, always ready to share the reason for our hope.

Evangelism is also an act of obedience to Christ's command. Luke 24:47-48 records Jesus' words to His disciples: "And that repentance and remission of sins should be preached in his name among all nations, beginning at Jerusalem. And ye are witnesses of these things." This commission is not optional but a direct command from our Lord, requiring us to share the Gospel proactively. Acts 20:24 reflects the apostle Paul's commitment to this mission: "But none of these things move me, neither count I my life dear unto myself, so that I might finish my course with joy, and the ministry, which I have received of the Lord Jesus, to testify the gospel of the grace of God." Paul's example challenges us to prioritize the mission of evangelism, even in the face of difficulties and sacrifices.

Furthermore, evangelism expresses our hope and assurance in God's promises. Romans 1:16 declares, "For I am not ashamed of the gospel of Christ: for it is the power of God unto salvation to every one that believeth; to the Jew first, and also to the Greek." This confidence in the Gospel's power to save motivates us to share it boldly and unashamedly. 1 Peter 3:15 encourages us to be prepared to share our faith continually: "But sanctify the Lord God in your hearts: and be ready always to give an answer to every man that asketh you a reason of the hope that is in you with meekness and fear." This readiness involves being knowledgeable about our faith and willing to engage in conversations about the Gospel.

Chapter 5 - Denouncing Sin

Authentic Christianity, the heart of old-time religion, strongly emphasizes speaking out against sin. This critical aspect of the faith is rooted in the belief that boldly addressing sin is necessary for living a life that honors God. Ephesians 5:11 admonishes, "And have no fellowship with the unfruitful works of darkness, but rather reprove them." This verse teaches us to avoid participating in sinful deeds and actively expose and correct them. This involves personal repentance and a commitment to stand against sinful practices in society, calling others to recognize their need for redemption through Jesus Christ.

God often calls His people to speak out against sin in the Bible. Proverbs 27:5 says, "Open rebuke is better than secret love." This means it is more loving and beneficial to openly correct someone's sinning than to condone their behavior silently. Speaking out against sin is an act of love because it helps others recognize their wrongdoing and return to God.

Isaiah 58:1 commands, "Cry aloud, spare not, lift up thy voice like a trumpet, and shew my people their transgression, and the house of Jacob their sins." This verse emphasizes the need to loudly declare the people's sins, urging them to repent and return to God. It highlights the responsibility of believers to confront sin and call for repentance, both in their own lives and in the lives of others.

In the New Testament, John the Baptist is a powerful example who boldly spoke out against sin. Matthew 3:1-2 records, "In those days came John the Baptist, preaching in the wilderness of Judaea, And saying, Repent ye: for the kingdom of heaven is at hand." John's message was clear and direct, urging people to repent of their sins in preparation for the coming of the Lord. His boldness in addressing sin ultimately cost him his life, but his commitment to truth and righteousness is an enduring example for all believers.

Jesus Himself spoke out against sin with authority and conviction. In Matthew 23, Jesus delivers a series of solid rebukes to the Pharisees and scribes, calling them out for their hypocrisy and sinful behavior. Matthew 23:27 says, "Woe unto you, scribes and Pharisees, hypocrites! for ye are like unto whited sepulchres, which indeed appear beautiful outward, but are within full of dead men's bones, and of all uncleanness." Jesus' willingness to confront sin head-on, even in the religious leaders of His time, demonstrates the importance of addressing sin boldly and truthfully.

Speaking out against sin also involves personal repentance. 1 John 1:8-9 teaches, "If we say that we have no sin, we deceive ourselves, and the truth is not in us. If we confess our sins, he is faithful and just to forgive us our sins, and to cleanse us from all unrighteousness." Acknowledging our sins and seeking God's forgiveness is crucial to the Christian life. Through this process of repentance and forgiveness, we are cleansed and made righteous before God.

In addition to personal repentance, old-time religion calls believers to stand against sinful practices in society. Romans 12:2 instructs, "And be not conformed to this world: but be ye transformed by the renewing of your mind, that ye may prove what is that good, and acceptable, and perfect, will of God." This verse encourages believers not to adopt the sinful ways of the world but to be transformed by God's Word, living in a way that pleases Him and serves as a testimony to others.

Believers must also be a light in a dark world. Matthew 5:14-16 says, "Ye are the light of the world. A city that is set on an hill cannot be hid. Neither do men light a candle, and put it under a bushel, but on a candlestick; and it giveth light unto all that are in the house. Let your light so shine before men, that they may see your good works, and glorify your Father which is in heaven." By living righteously and speaking out against sin, Christians can shine the light of God's truth into a dark and sinful world, guiding others to Him.

Ephesians 4:29-30 instructs, "Let no corrupt communication proceed out of your mouth, but that which is good to the use of edifying, that it may minister grace unto the hearers. And grieve not the holy

Spirit of God, whereby ye are sealed unto the day of redemption." We should use our words to build up and encourage others, speak truth in love, and help lead them away from sin. It is essential to address sin in a way that reflects God's grace and compassion, always aiming to restore and redeem.

Believers must also intercede for those caught in sin. James 5:19-20 says, "Brethren, if any of you do err from the truth, and one convert him; Let him know, that he which converteth the sinner from the error of his way shall save a soul from death, and shall hide a multitude of sins." This verse highlights the importance of helping others turn away from sin and back to God, emphasizing the eternal significance of such actions.

The Bible also warns of the dangers of tolerating sin within the church. 1 Corinthians 5:6-7 states, "Your glorying is not good. Know ye not that a little leaven leaveneth the whole lump? Purge out therefore the old leaven, that ye may be a new lump, as ye are unleavened. For even Christ our passover is sacrificed for us." This passage teaches that tolerating sin can corrupt the entire community, and it is essential to address and remove sin to maintain the purity and holiness of the church.

Galatians 6:1-2 instructs, "Brethren, if a man be overtaken in a fault, ye which are spiritual, restore such an one in the spirit of meekness; considering thyself, lest thou also be tempted. Bear ye one another's burdens, and so fulfil the law of Christ." This passage emphasizes the importance of restoring those who have fallen into sin with gentleness and humility, recognizing our vulnerability to temptation. By supporting and encouraging one another, we fulfill the law of Christ, which is to love one another as He has loved us.

Believers must also be bold in their witness, even in the face of opposition. Acts 4:18-20 recounts the boldness of Peter and John: "And they called them, and commanded them not to speak at all nor teach in the name of Jesus. But Peter and John answered and said unto them, Whether it be right in the sight of God to hearken unto you more than unto God, judge ye. For we cannot but speak the things which we have seen and heard." This example shows that speaking out against sin and proclaiming the truth of the Gospel is more important than seeking the approval of others or avoiding conflict.

In addressing sin, it is crucial to remember the ultimate goal: to lead people to repentance and reconciliation with God. 2 Corinthians 5:18-20 explains, "And all things are of God, who hath reconciled us to himself by Jesus Christ, and hath given to us the ministry of reconciliation; To wit, that God was in Christ, reconciling the world unto himself, not imputing their trespasses unto them; and hath committed unto us the word of reconciliation. Now then we are ambassadors for Christ, as though God did beseech you by us: we pray you in Christ's stead, be ye reconciled to God." We should always aim our efforts to speak out against sin and help others find forgiveness and restoration through Jesus Christ.

In summary, authentic Christianity, the heart of old-time religion, strongly emphasizes speaking out against sin. This involves personal repentance and a commitment to stand against sinful societal practices, calling others to recognize their need for redemption. We are called to address sin boldly, following the examples of biblical figures like John the Baptist and Jesus, who confronted sin with authority and conviction. Our words and actions should reflect God's truth and love, guiding others away from sin and towards a relationship with Him. By living righteously, supporting one another, and boldly proclaiming the Gospel, we can shine the light of God's truth into a dark world and help lead others to salvation and transformation in Jesus Christ. This commitment to addressing sin and calling for repentance is a fundamental aspect of old-time religion and the foundation of authentic Christianity.

Chapter 6 - Delivering the Message of the Saviour

Authentic Christianity, the heart of old-time religion, emphasizes telling the sinner about the Savior, rooted in the message of salvation through Jesus Christ. This core belief is anchored in the understanding that humanity needs redemption due to sin, and God has provided a way through His Son, Jesus Christ. Romans 5:8 proclaims, "But God commendeth his love toward us, in that, while we were yet sinners, Christ died for us." This powerful verse encapsulates the essence of the Gospel—the sacrificial love of God demonstrated through the death of Jesus Christ on the cross for the forgiveness of our sins. Sharing this message is a responsibility and a profound act of love and obedience to God's command.

The foundation of this message begins with recognizing sin and its consequences. Romans 3:23 states, "For all have sinned, and come short of the glory of God." This verse clarifies that everyone has sinned and requires God's grace. Romans 6:23 further explains the consequence of sin, stating, "For the wages of sin is death; but the gift of God is eternal life through Jesus Christ our Lord." This highlights the dire outcome of sin—spiritual death—but also points to the hope and gift of eternal life available through Jesus Christ.

Central to the old-time religion is the belief in the sacrificial death and resurrection of Jesus Christ as the only means of salvation. John 3:16, one of the Bible's most well-known and cherished verses, declares, "For God so loved the world, that he gave his only begotten Son, that whosoever believeth in him should not perish, but have everlasting life." This verse underscores God's immense love and desire to save humanity. It also emphasizes that belief in Jesus Christ is the key to receiving eternal life.

Telling the sinner about the Savior involves sharing the story of Jesus' death and resurrection. This narrative is central to the Christian faith and is the cornerstone of the Gospel message. 1 Corinthians 15:3-4 provides a summary of this message: "For I delivered unto you first of all that which I also received, how that Christ died for our sins according to the scriptures; And that he was buried, and that he rose again the third day according to the scriptures." This passage highlights the fundamental truths that Jesus died for our sins, was buried, and rose again on the third day, per the Scriptures.

Sharing the Gospel is an act of obedience to the Great Commission given by Jesus Christ. In Matthew 28:19-20, Jesus commands His followers, "Go ye therefore, and teach all nations, baptizing them in the name of the Father, and of the Son, and of the Holy Ghost: Teaching them to observe all things whatsoever I have commanded you: and, lo, I am with you alway, even unto the end of the world." This directive emphasizes the importance of spreading the message of salvation to all people, making disciples, baptizing them, and teaching them to follow Jesus' teachings.

The motivation for sharing the Gospel is rooted in the love of Christ and a desire to see others experience the same salvation and transformation we have received. 2 Corinthians 5:14-15 explains, "For the love of Christ constraineth us; because we thus judge, that if one died for all, then were all dead: And that he died for all, that they which live should not henceforth live unto themselves, but unto him which died for them, and rose again." This passage highlights that Christ's love compels us to share the Gospel, recognizing that Jesus died for everyone and that those who live should live for Him.

The book of Acts shows numerous examples of early Christians boldly sharing Jesus' message. Acts 4:12 states, "Neither is there salvation in any other: for there is none other name under heaven given among men, whereby we must be saved." This verse emphasizes the exclusivity of salvation through Jesus Christ, underscoring that He is the only way to be saved. The apostles and early believers were passionate about proclaiming this truth, even in the face of persecution and opposition.

Sharing the Gospel involves proclaiming the message and calling people to respond. Acts 2:38 records Peter's response to those convicted by his message: "Then Peter said unto them, Repent, and be baptized every one of you in the name of Jesus Christ for the remission of sins, and ye shall receive the gift of the Holy Ghost." This call to repentance highlights the need for a personal response to the Gospel message, turning away from sin and placing faith in Jesus Christ.

The message of salvation through Jesus Christ also brings hope and assurance. Romans 10:9-10 promises, "That if thou shalt confess with thy mouth the Lord Jesus, and shalt believe in thine heart that God hath raised him from the dead, thou shalt be saved. For with the heart man believeth unto righteousness; and with the mouth confession is made unto salvation." This passage assures us that salvation is available to anyone who believes in their heart and confesses with their mouth that Jesus is Lord.

Sharing the Gospel is not just for trained ministers or evangelists but is a responsibility for all believers. 1 Peter 3:15 instructs, "But sanctify the Lord God in your hearts: and be ready always to give an answer to every man that asketh you a reason of the hope that is in you with meekness and fear." Every Christian is called to be prepared to share the reason for their hope to explain the message of Jesus with gentleness and respect.

Moreover, telling the sinner about the Savior involves living out the Gospel daily. Matthew 5:16 encourages us, "Let your light so shine before men, that they may see your good works, and glorify your Father which is in heaven." Our actions and lifestyle should reflect the Gospel's transforming power, serving as a testimony to others of God's love and grace. Philippians 2:15-16 urges believers to live blamelessly and shine as lights in the world, "That ye may be blameless and harmless, the sons of God, without rebuke, in the midst of a crooked and perverse nation, among whom ye shine as lights in the world; Holding forth the word of life." Our conduct should align with the message we proclaim, demonstrating the truth and power of the Gospel.

In addition to personal evangelism, the church plays a crucial role in spreading the message of salvation. Ephesians 4:11-12 describes the various roles within the church, "And he gave some, apostles; and some, prophets; and some, evangelists; and some, pastors and teachers; For the perfecting of the saints, for the work of the ministry, for the edifying of the body of Christ." The church must equip believers for ministry, build up the body of Christ, and work together to spread the Gospel.

Prayer is also a vital component of evangelism. Colossians 4:2-4 emphasizes the importance of prayer in sharing the Gospel, "Continue in prayer, and watch in the same with thanksgiving; Withal praying also for us, that God would open unto us a door of utterance, to speak the mystery of Christ, for which I am also in bonds: That I may make it manifest, as I ought to speak." This passage encourages believers to pray for opportunities to share the Gospel and for the boldness and clarity to proclaim it effectively.

The message of salvation through Jesus Christ is also a message of reconciliation. 2 Corinthians 5:18-19 explains, "And all things are of God, who hath reconciled us to himself by Jesus Christ, and hath given to us the ministry of reconciliation; To wit, that God was in Christ, reconciling the world unto himself, not imputing their trespasses unto them; and hath committed unto us the word of reconciliation." This passage highlights that through Jesus, God is reconciling the world to Himself, not counting people's sins against them and that we are entrusted with this message of reconciliation.

The reality of eternity underscores the urgency of sharing the Gospel. Hebrews 9:27-28 states, "And as it is appointed unto men once to die, but after this the judgment: So Christ was once offered to bear the sins of many; and unto them that look for him shall he appear the second time without sin unto salvation." This passage reminds us that every person will face judgment after death, and the opportunity to accept salvation is limited to this life. This urgency compels us to share the message of Jesus with diligence and compassion.

The assurance of salvation through Jesus Christ brings peace and joy. Romans 5:1 declares, "Therefore being justified by faith, we have peace with God through our Lord Jesus Christ." This peace with God made possible through faith in Jesus, is a central aspect of the Gospel message. Additionally, the joy of salvation is expressed in 1 Peter 1:8-9, "Whom having not seen, ye love; in whom, though now ye see him not, yet believing, ye rejoice with joy unspeakable and full of glory: Receiving the end of your faith, even the salvation of your souls." This joy and assurance result from a genuine relationship with Jesus Christ and are critical elements of the message we share with others.

In summary, authentic Christianity, the heart of old-time religion, places a central emphasis on telling the sinner about the Savior. This involves sharing the story of Jesus' sacrificial death and resurrection, highlighting His love and the hope He offers. The message of salvation through Jesus Christ is rooted in recognizing sin, the need for redemption, the proclamation of Jesus' death and resurrection, and the call to repentance and faith. Obedience to the Great Commission, motivated by the love of Christ and compassion for the lost, drives us to engage in personal evangelism and collective efforts within the church. The assurance of salvation brings peace and joy, compelling us to share this message with urgency and passion. By telling the sinner about the Savior, we fulfill our calling as followers of Jesus and bring glory to God, the source of our salvation.

Chapter 7 - Devotion to the Atoning Blood of Christ

Authentic Christianity, the heart of old-time religion, centers on faith in the atoning blood of Jesus Christ, which is critical for understanding the true essence of salvation. Belief in the saving power of Jesus' shed blood is fundamental because it affirms that Christ's blood forgives sins and makes reconciliation with God possible. Hebrews 9:22 states, "And almost all things are by the law purged with blood; and without shedding of blood is no remission." This verse underscores the necessity of blood for the forgiveness of sins. This truth is deeply rooted in the sacrificial system of the Old Testament and perfectly fulfilled in the New Testament through Jesus Christ.

The significance of Jesus' blood is seen throughout the Scriptures, beginning with the sacrificial practices in the Old Testament. Leviticus 17:11 explains, "For the life of the flesh is in the blood: and I have given it to you upon the altar to make an atonement for your souls: for it is the blood that maketh an atonement for the soul." This principle established the understanding that life, represented by blood, is required to atone for sin. However, the blood of animals was insufficient for the complete removal of sin; it pointed to the ultimate sacrifice of Jesus Christ. John the Baptist recognized this when he saw Jesus and declared in John 1:29, "Behold the Lamb of God, which taketh away the sin of the world."

The New Testament further clarifies the importance of Jesus' blood in the new covenant context. Jesus Himself emphasized this during the Last Supper, as recorded in Matthew 26:28, "For this is my blood of the new testament, which is shed for many for the remission of sins." Here, Jesus explains that His blood is the foundation of the new covenant, shed for forgiving sins. "By shedding His blood on the cross, Jesus made the ultimate sacrifice, fulfilling the law's requirements and providing the way for humanity to be reconciled with God."

The apostle Paul also highlights the critical role of Jesus' blood in salvation. Romans 5:9 states, "Much more then, being now justified by his blood, we shall be saved from wrath through him." This verse teaches that believers are justified, or declared righteous, by the blood of Jesus, which saves them from the wrath of God. Additionally, Ephesians 1:7 affirms, "In whom we have redemption through his blood, the forgiveness of sins, according to the riches of his grace." This passage emphasizes that redemption and forgiveness are made possible through the blood of Jesus, showcasing the richness of God's grace.

The concept of reconciliation with God through Jesus' blood is also vividly presented in Colossians 1:20, "And, having made peace through the blood of his cross, by him to reconcile all things unto himself." This verse shows that peace with God and the reconciliation of all things are achieved through the blood of Jesus shed on the cross. It highlights Christ's sacrifice's transformative power, bridging the gap between sinful humanity and a holy God.

The book of Hebrews thoroughly explains the superiority of Jesus' sacrifice over the old sacrificial system. Hebrews 9:12 states, "Neither by the blood of goats and calves, but by his own blood he entered in once into the holy place, having obtained eternal redemption for us." This verse contrasts the repeated sacrifices of animals with the once-for-all sacrifice of Jesus, whose blood secured eternal redemption. Furthermore, Hebrews 10:19-20 encourages believers, "Having therefore, brethren, boldness to enter into the holiest by the blood of Jesus, By a new and living way, which he hath consecrated for us, through the veil, that is to say, his flesh." This passage underscores that it is through Jesus' blood that believers have bold access to God's presence, a privilege previously unavailable under the old covenant.

The book of Revelation also emphasizes the power and significance of Jesus' blood. Revelation 1:5 declares, "And from Jesus Christ, who is the faithful witness, and the first begotten of the dead, and the prince of the kings of the earth. Unto him that loved us, and washed us from our sins in his own blood." This verse highlights the love of Jesus and the cleansing power of His blood, which washes away sins. Revelation 12:11 further states, "And they overcame him by the blood of the Lamb, and by the word of their testimony; and they loved not their lives unto the death." This passage reveals that believers overcome the accuser, Satan, by the blood of the Lamb and their testimony, showing the victorious power of Christ's blood in the life of a Christian.

Faith in the atoning blood of Jesus Christ also brings assurance of salvation and eternal life. 1 Peter 1:18-19 reassures believers, "Forasmuch as ye know that ye were not redeemed with corruptible things, as silver and gold, from your vain conversation received by tradition from your fathers; But with the precious blood of Christ, as of a lamb without blemish and without spot." This passage underscores the invaluable nature of Christ's blood, which is far more precious than any earthly wealth and is the means of our redemption.

The power of Jesus' blood to cleanse from sin is a recurring theme in the New Testament. 1 John 1:7 affirms, "But if we walk in the light, as he is in the light, we have fellowship one with another, and the blood of Jesus Christ his Son cleanseth us from all sin." This verse teaches that as believers walk in the light, in fellowship with God and one another, the blood of Jesus continually cleanses them from all sin. This ongoing cleansing is essential for maintaining a close relationship with God and living a holy life.

Moreover, the blood of Jesus is central to the believer's sanctification process. Hebrews 13:12 explains, "Wherefore Jesus also, that he might sanctify the people with his own blood, suffered without the gate." This verse highlights that Jesus' suffering and the shedding of His blood sanctify, or set apart, believers for God. This sanctification process involves being made holy and living a life that reflects God's character.

The belief in the atoning blood of Jesus Christ also provides a basis for unity among believers. Ephesians 2:13 states, "But now in Christ Jesus ye who sometimes were far off are made nigh by the blood of Christ." This verse teaches that Jesus' blood brings those once far from God near, creating a unified body of believers. This unity is based on the shared experience of being redeemed by the same precious blood of Jesus.

The sacrificial death of Jesus and the shedding of His blood were also prophesied in the Old Testament, pointing to the fulfillment of God's redemptive plan. Isaiah 53:5 prophesies, "But he was wounded for our transgressions, he was bruised for our iniquities: the chastisement of our peace was upon him; and with his stripes we are healed." This prophetic verse foretells the suffering and sacrifice of Jesus, emphasizing that His wounds and shed blood bring healing and peace to humanity.

Faith in the atoning blood of Jesus is also foundational for the believer's confidence in approaching God. Hebrews 4:16 encourages, "Let us therefore come boldly unto the throne of grace, that we may obtain mercy, and find grace to help in time of need." This confidence is rooted in the knowledge that Jesus' blood has allowed believers to enter God's presence with boldness, assured of His mercy and grace.

The recognition of the atoning power of Jesus' blood inspires gratitude and worship. Revelation 5:9 records the praise of the heavenly hosts, "And they sung a new song, saying, Thou art worthy to take the book, and to open the seals thereof: for thou wast slain, and hast redeemed us to God by thy blood out of every kindred, and tongue, and people, and nation." This verse highlights the worship directed towards Jesus for His sacrificial death and the redemption He accomplished through His blood, drawing people from every nation to God.

In summary, authentic Christianity, the heart of old-time religion, emphasizes faith in the atoning blood of Jesus Christ. The belief in the saving power of Jesus' shed blood is critical because it affirms that sins are forgiven through Christ's blood and reconciliation with God is made possible. Hebrews 9:22 underscores the necessity of blood for the forgiveness of sins, a concept deeply rooted in the sacrificial system of the Old Testament and perfectly fulfilled in the New Testament through Jesus Christ. The significance of the blood of Jesus is seen throughout the Scriptures, from the sacrificial practices in the Old Testament to the ultimate sacrifice of Jesus on the cross, providing a way for humanity to be reconciled with God. The New Testament further clarifies the importance of Jesus' blood in the new covenant context. Jesus emphasizes that His blood is the foundation of the new covenant, shed for forgiving sins. The apostle Paul and other New Testament writers highlight the critical role of Jesus' blood in salvation, justification, redemption, and reconciliation. The book of Hebrews explains the superiority of Jesus' sacrifice over the old sacrificial system, emphasizing that it is through Jesus' blood that believers have bold access to the presence of God. The book of Revelation emphasizes the power and significance of Jesus' blood, highlighting its cleansing, overcoming, and unifying power. Faith in the atoning blood of Jesus Christ brings assurance of salvation, eternal life, ongoing cleansing from sin, and sanctification. It also provides unity among believers and confidence in approaching God. The recognition of the atoning power of Jesus' blood inspires gratitude and worship as believers acknowledge the immense love and sacrifice of Jesus for their redemption.

Chapter 8 - Defeat of Death by Jesus Christ

Authentic Christianity, the heart of old-time religion, places a foundational emphasis on Jesus Christ's resurrection, a cornerstone of the Christian faith. The resurrection is central to the message of the Gospel and assures future resurrection and eternal life for all who believe. 1 Corinthians 15:3-4 affirms, "For I delivered unto you first of all that which I also received, how that Christ died for our sins according to the scriptures; And that he was buried, and that he rose again the third day according to the scriptures." This passage underscores the importance of Jesus' death, burial, and resurrection, which fulfill the prophecies and promises of the Scriptures. The resurrection is not just an event in history but a pivotal moment that validates Jesus' divinity, His victory over sin and death, and the hope of eternal life for believers.

The resurrection of Jesus Christ is the defining moment that sets Christianity apart from all other religions. Romans 1:4 declares, "And declared to be the Son of God with power, according to the spirit of holiness, by the resurrection from the dead." This verse emphasizes that the resurrection confirms Jesus as the Son of God, demonstrating His divine power and authority. The resurrection is the ultimate proof that Jesus is who He claimed to be: the world's Messiah and Saviour.

The resurrection also assures believers of their justification. Romans 4:25 explains, "Who was delivered for our offences, and was raised again for our justification." This verse highlights that Jesus' resurrection was necessary for our justification, meaning that believers are declared righteous before God through His resurrection. The resurrection is the divine affirmation that Jesus' sacrifice was sufficient to atone for our sins and that through faith in Him, we are justified.

The believer's hope for future resurrection is intricately linked to Jesus' resurrection. 1 Corinthians 15:20-22 states, "But now is Christ risen from the dead, and become the firstfruits of them that slept. For since by man came death, by man came also the resurrection of the dead. For as in Adam all die, even so in Christ shall all be made alive." This passage teaches that Jesus' resurrection is the firstfruits, guaranteeing the future resurrection of all who belong to Him. Just as death came through Adam, resurrection, and life come through Jesus Christ. This assurance of future resurrection gives believers hope and confidence in the promise of eternal life.

The resurrection is also essential for the believer's new life in Christ. Romans 6:4 states, "Therefore we are buried with him by baptism into death: that like as Christ was raised up from the dead by the glory of the Father, even so we also should walk in newness of life." This verse emphasizes that just as Jesus was raised from the dead, believers are raised to walk in the newness of life. Jesus' resurrection power transforms believers, enabling them to live a new life of righteousness and holiness. The resurrection of Jesus Christ is also a source of comfort and encouragement for believers facing trials and persecution. 1 Peter 1:3-4 says, "Blessed be the God and Father of our Lord Jesus Christ, which according to his abundant mercy hath begotten us again unto a lively hope by the resurrection of Jesus Christ from the dead, To an inheritance incorruptible, and undefiled, and that fadeth not away, reserved in heaven for you." This passage highlights that the resurrection gives believers a living hope and assures them of an eternal inheritance that is imperishable, undefiled, and unfading. The certainty of this hope sustains believers through difficulties, knowing that their ultimate reward is secure in heaven.

The resurrection also provides the basis for the believer's victory over sin and death. 1 Corinthians 15:55-57 proclaims, "O death, where is thy sting? O grave, where is thy victory? The sting of death is sin; and the strength of sin is the law. But thanks be to God, which giveth us the victory through our Lord Jesus Christ." This passage celebrates the victory over death and sin through the resurrection of Jesus Christ. Believers can face death without fear, knowing that Jesus has conquered the grave and that they share in His victory.

The reality of the resurrection also compels believers to live with eternal perspective and purpose. Colossians 3:1-2 instructs, "If ye then be risen with Christ, seek those things which are above, where Christ sitteth on the right hand of God. Set your affection on things above, not on things on the earth." This passage encourages believers to focus on heavenly things, living in light of their resurrection with Christ and their future hope. The resurrection motivates believers to prioritize their lives according to God's eternal purposes rather than temporary earthly concerns.

Furthermore, the resurrection is a crucial element in the proclamation of the Gospel. Acts 4:33 records, "And with great power gave the apostles witness of the resurrection of the Lord Jesus: and great grace was upon them all." The apostles boldly proclaimed the resurrection of Jesus as central to their message, and it was through this testimony that many came to faith. The resurrection is the cornerstone of the Christian faith, and through this message, the power of the Gospel is made known.

The resurrection also assures believers of Jesus' ongoing intercession and advocacy. Romans 8:34 declares, "Who is he that condemneth? It is Christ that died, yea rather, that is risen again, who is even at the right hand of God, who also maketh intercession for us." This verse highlights that Jesus, who is risen and ascended to the right hand of God, continually intercedes for believers. His resurrection ensures that He is alive and actively working on behalf of His people, providing them with ongoing support and advocacy before the Father.

Additionally, the resurrection of Jesus Christ demonstrates God's power and faithfulness. Ephesians 1:19-20 speaks of "the exceeding greatness of his power to us-ward who believe, according to the working of his mighty power, Which he wrought in Christ, when he raised him from the dead, and set him at his own right hand in the heavenly places." This passage emphasizes that the same power that raised Jesus from the dead is at work in believers, assuring them of God's ability to fulfill His promises and sustain them in their faith.

The resurrection also signifies the defeat of Satan and his forces. Colossians 2:15 declares, "And having spoiled principalities and powers, he made a shew of them openly, triumphing over them in it." This verse highlights that Jesus triumphed over the powers of darkness through His death and resurrection, disarming them and publicly displaying His victory. Believers can live confidently, knowing that Satan's defeat was accomplished through the resurrection of Jesus Christ.

The resurrection also demonstrates God's love and commitment to His creation. John 11:25-26 records Jesus' words, "I am the resurrection, and the life: he that believeth in me, though he were dead, yet shall he live: And whosoever liveth and believeth in me shall never die. Believest thou this?" This passage reveals Jesus as the source of resurrection and life, offering eternal life to all who believe in Him. The resurrection is a testament to God's desire to restore life and bring His people into an everlasting relationship with Him.

Moreover, the resurrection of Jesus Christ provides the foundation for Christian hope. 1 Thessalonians 4:14 offers comfort to believers mourning the loss of loved ones, "For if we believe that Jesus died and rose again, even so them also which sleep in Jesus will God bring with him." This verse reassures believers that just as Jesus was raised from the dead, those who have died in Christ will also be raised and reunited with Him. The resurrection offers hope and assures that death is not the end but the beginning of eternal life with God.

The resurrection also calls believers to a life of obedience and holiness. Romans 6:5-6 states, "For if we have been planted together in the likeness of his death, we shall be also in the likeness of his resurrection: Knowing this, that our old man is crucified with him, that the body of sin might be destroyed, that henceforth we should not serve sin." This passage teaches that believers united with Christ in His death and resurrection are called to live a new life free from the bondage of sin. The resurrection empowers believers to live in obedience to God and pursue holiness.

In summary, authentic Christianity, the heart of old-time religion, places a foundational emphasis on Jesus Christ's resurrection, a cornerstone of the Christian faith. The resurrection is central to the message of the Gospel and assures future resurrection and eternal life for all who believe. 1 Corinthians 15:3-4 underscores the importance of Jesus' death, burial, and resurrection, fulfilling the prophecies and promises of the Scriptures. The resurrection confirms Jesus as the Son of God, assures believers of their justification, and guarantees their future resurrection. It empowers believers to live a new life in Christ, provides comfort and encouragement in trials, and assures victory over sin and death. The resurrection also compels believers to live with eternal perspective and purpose, motivates the proclamation of the Gospel, and assures Jesus' ongoing intercession and advocacy. It demonstrates God's power, faithfulness, and love, signifies the defeat of Satan, and provides the foundation for Christian hope. The resurrection calls believers to a life of obedience and holiness, empowering them to live in righteousness and pursue a life that reflects God's character. This emphasis on the resurrection of Jesus Christ is central to the message and mission of authentic Christianity, the heart of old-time religion.

Chapter 9 - - Dialogue and Communion with God

Authentic Christianity, the heart of old-time religion, emphasizes prayer and communion with God, essential for maintaining a robust and vibrant spiritual life. 1 Thessalonians 5:17 encourages believers to "Pray without ceasing." This verse emphasizes the importance of constant and continual prayer, highlighting it as a vital means of maintaining a close relationship with God, seeking His guidance, confessing sins, and interceding for others. Prayer is constant communication with God, reflecting a deep and abiding relationship.

Prayer is the lifeline of a believer's spiritual life. Philippians 4:6-7 instructs, "Be careful for nothing; but in every thing by prayer and supplication with thanksgiving let your requests be made known unto God. And the peace of God, which passeth all understanding, shall keep your hearts and minds through Christ Jesus." This passage teaches that through prayer, believers can bring all their concerns and needs to God with thanksgiving, and in return, they will experience His peace, which transcends human understanding. This peace guards their hearts and minds, providing comfort and assurance amid life's challenges.

In the model prayer given by Jesus, commonly known as the Lord's Prayer, He provides a comprehensive framework for prayer. Matthew 6:9-13 says, "After this manner therefore pray ye: Our Father which art in heaven, Hallowed be thy name. Thy kingdom come. Thy will be done in earth, as it is in heaven. Give us this day our daily bread. And forgive us our debts, as we forgive our debtors. And lead us not into temptation, but deliver us from evil: For thine is the kingdom, and the power, and the glory, for ever. Amen." This prayer encompasses adoration, submission to God's will, provision, forgiveness, and deliverance from evil, serving as a model for how believers should approach God in prayer.

Prayer is also a means of seeking God's guidance and wisdom. James 1:5 encourages, "If any of you lack wisdom, let him ask of God, that giveth to all men liberally, and upbraideth not; and it shall be given him." This verse assures believers that when they seek God's wisdom through prayer, He will generously provide it without reproach. This highlights the importance of prayer in decision-making and seeking direction in life.

Confessing sins and seeking forgiveness is another crucial aspect of prayer. 1 John 1:9 promises, "If we confess our sins, he is faithful and just to forgive us our sins, and to cleanse us from all unrighteousness." This verse emphasizes that through prayer, believers can confess their sins and receive God's forgiveness and cleansing. This process of confession and forgiveness is essential for maintaining a pure and unblemished relationship with God. Intercession, or praying on behalf of others, is also a significant aspect of prayer. 1 Timothy 2:1-2 urges, "I exhort therefore, that, first of all, supplications, prayers, intercessions, and giving of thanks, be made for all men; For kings, and for all that are in authority; that we may lead a quiet and peaceable life in all godliness and honesty." This passage encourages believers to pray for all people, including those in positions of authority, highlighting the importance of intercessory prayer in promoting peace and godliness in society.

The life of Jesus provides numerous examples of the importance of prayer. Mark 1:35 records, "And in the morning, rising up a great while before day, he went out, and departed into a solitary place, and there prayed." Jesus often withdrew to solitary places to pray, demonstrating the necessity of setting aside time for focused and intimate communication with God. Luke 5:16 notes, "And he withdrew himself into the wilderness, and prayed." These examples from Jesus' life underscore His priority on prayer and His intimate communion with the Father.

The early church also exemplified the importance of prayer in the life of believers. Acts 2:42 describes the early Christians, "And they continued stedfastly in the apostles' doctrine and fellowship, and in breaking of bread, and in prayers." The early church devoted themselves to prayer, teaching, fellowship, and breaking bread, showing that prayer was a central and foundational practice in their communal and spiritual life.

Prayer is also a source of strength and encouragement in times of trouble. Psalm 34:17 assures, "The righteous cry, and the LORD heareth, and delivereth them out of all their troubles." This verse highlights that God hears the prayers of the righteous and delivers them from their troubles, providing comfort and hope in difficult times. Philippians 4:13 strengthens believers by affirming, "I can do all things through Christ which strengtheneth me." Through prayer, believers receive strength and empowerment from Christ to face life's challenges.

The book of Psalms contains prayers expressing a wide range of emotions, from praise and thanksgiving to lament and supplication. Psalm 55:17 says, "Evening, and morning, and at noon, will I pray, and cry aloud: and he shall hear my voice." This verse reflects the psalmist's commitment to continual prayer throughout the day, trusting that God hears and responds to his cries. Psalm 145:18 declares, "The LORD is nigh unto all them that call upon him, to all that call upon him in truth." This verse assures believers that God is near to all who call on Him in truth, emphasizing His readiness to listen and respond to their prayers.

Prayer is also an expression of faith and trust in God. Hebrews 11:6 teaches, "But without faith it is impossible to please him: for he that cometh to God must believe that he is, and that he is a rewarder of them that diligently seek him." This verse emphasizes that approaching God in prayer requires faith, believing in His existence, and His willingness to reward those who earnestly seek Him. Prayer is an act of faith that demonstrates dependence on God and trust in His character and promises.

In addition to individual prayer, corporate prayer is essential to the Christian faith. Matthew 18:19-20 states, "Again I say unto you, That if two of you shall agree on earth as touching any thing that they shall ask, it shall be done for them of my Father which is in heaven. For where two or three are gathered together in my name, there am I in the midst of them." This passage highlights the power and significance of believers coming together in prayer, agreeing in faith, and experiencing the presence of Jesus in their midst. Fasting, combined with prayer, is also an assertive spiritual discipline. Matthew 6:17-18 instructs, "But thou, when thou fastest, anoint thine head, and wash thy face; That thou appear not unto men to fast, but unto thy Father which is in secret: and thy Father, which seeth in secret, shall reward thee openly." When done with the right heart and motive, fasting enhances the prayer experience, helping believers focus more intently on God and His purposes.

Prayer also plays a vital role in spiritual warfare. Ephesians 6:18 exhorts, "Praying always with all prayer and supplication in the Spirit, and watching thereunto with all perseverance and supplication for all saints." This verse encourages believers to be vigilant and persistent in prayer, recognizing that it is a crucial weapon in their spiritual battles. By praying in the Spirit and interceding for fellow believers, they stand firm against the enemy's schemes.

The transformative power of prayer is evident throughout the Bible. James 5:16 declares, "Confess your faults one to another, and pray one for another, that ye may be healed. The effectual fervent prayer of a righteous man availeth much." This verse emphasizes the effectiveness of fervent prayer offered by a righteous person, highlighting its power to bring about healing and change.

Prayer also deepens the believer's relationship with God, fostering intimacy and fellowship. Psalm 63:1 expresses the psalmist's longing for God, "O God, thou art my God; early will I seek thee: my soul thirsteth for thee, my flesh longeth for thee in a dry and thirsty land, where no water is." This verse reflects the deep desire and yearning for God's presence cultivated through prayer. Prayer is a means of drawing near to God and experiencing His presence profoundly and personally.

The promise of answered prayer is another encouragement for believers to maintain a robust prayer life. Matthew 7:7-8 assures, "Ask, and it shall be given you; seek, and ye shall find; knock, and it shall be opened unto you: For every one that asketh receiveth; and he that seeketh findeth; and to him that knocketh it shall be opened." This passage encourages believers to pray with the assurance that God hears and answers their requests.

Jesus illustrates the importance of persistence in prayer through the parable of the persistent widow. Luke 18:1-8 narrates, "And he spake a parable unto them to this end, that men ought always to pray, and not to faint; Saying, There was in a city a judge, which feared not God, neither regarded man: And there was a widow in that city; and she came unto him, saying, Avenge me of mine adversary. And he would not for a while: but afterward he said within himself, Though I fear not God, nor regard man; Yet because this widow troubleth me, I will avenge her, lest by her continual coming she weary me. And the Lord said, Hear what the unjust judge saith. And shall not God avenge his own elect, which cry day and night unto him, though he bear long with them? I tell you that he will avenge them speedily. Nevertheless when the Son of man cometh, shall he find faith on the earth?" This parable encourages believers to pray and not lose heart, trusting God to respond to their cries.

In summary, authentic Christianity, the heart of old-time religion, strongly emphasizes prayer and communion with God, essential for maintaining a robust and vibrant spiritual life. 1 Thessalonians 5:17 encourages believers to "Pray without ceasing." Prayer is vital to maintaining a close relationship with God, seeking His guidance, confessing sins, and interceding for others. Prayer is the lifeline of a believer's spiritual life, providing peace, strength, and advice. The model prayer given by Jesus, known as the Lord's Prayer, encompasses adoration, submission to God's will, provision, forgiveness, and deliverance from evil. Seeking God's wisdom, confessing sins, and interceding for others are crucial aspects of prayer. The life of Jesus and the early church exemplify the importance of prayer, with Jesus often withdrawing to pray and the early Christians devoting themselves to prayer. Prayer provides strength and encouragement in times of trouble, with the Psalms expressing a wide range of emotions in prayer. Prayer expresses faith and trust in God, with corporate prayer being powerful and significant. Fasting, combined with prayer, enhances the prayer experience, while prayer plays a vital role in spiritual warfare. The transformative power of prayer brings healing and change, deepening the believer's relationship with God. The promise of answered prayer encourages persistence in prayer, as illustrated in the parable of the persistent widow. By maintaining a robust prayer life, believers cultivate a deep and abiding relationship with God, experiencing His presence, guidance, and power. This emphasis on prayer and communion with God is central to the message and mission of authentic Christianity, the heart of old-time religion.

Chapter 10 - - Dedicated and Devout Living

Authentic Christianity, the heart of old-time religion, emphasizes holiness and righteous living, calling for holiness and separation from the world's sinful influences. This commitment is based on the teaching of 1 Peter 1:15-16, which states, "But as he which hath called you is holy, so be ye holy in all manner of conversation; Because it is written, Be ye holy; for I am holy." This verse underscores the necessity for believers to strive to live in a way that reflects God's purity and righteousness, emphasizing that holiness is not just an abstract concept but a practical call to action in every aspect of life.

Living a life of holiness involves being set apart for God's purposes and avoiding the sinful practices that characterize the world. Romans 12:2 instructs, "And be not conformed to this world: but be ye transformed by the renewing of your mind, that ye may prove what is that good, and acceptable, and perfect, will of God." This verse highlights the need for believers to resist conforming to the patterns of this world and instead be transformed by renewing their minds. This transformation enables believers to discern and live out God's will, which is good, acceptable, and perfect.

The call to holiness is rooted in the nature of God Himself. Leviticus 19:2 commands, "Speak unto all the congregation of the children of Israel, and say unto them, Ye shall be holy: for I the LORD your God am holy." This Old Testament command reflects the continuity of God's call for His people to be holy based on His divine nature. The New Testament echoes this call, emphasizing that holiness is integral to the believer's identity and conduct.

Living a holy and righteous life involves avoiding sin and actively pursuing righteousness. 2 Timothy 2:22 advises, "Flee also youthful lusts: but follow righteousness, faith, charity, peace, with them that call on the Lord out of a pure heart." This verse instructs believers to flee from sinful desires and pursue righteousness, faith, love, and peace alongside others who seek to live a pure life before God. This dual approach of avoiding sin and pursuing righteousness is essential for living a holy life.

Holiness also involves the concept of sanctification, which is the process of being made holy. 1 Thessalonians 4:3-4 states, "For this is the will of God, even your sanctification, that ye should abstain from fornication: That every one of you should know how to possess his vessel in sanctification and honor." This passage emphasizes that God's will for believers is their sanctification, which involves abstaining from sexual immorality and living in a way that honors God. Sanctification is an ongoing process that requires growth in holiness and deeper conformity to the image of Christ.

The Bible provides practical guidelines for holy living, emphasizing the importance of moral purity, integrity, and godly conduct. Philippians 4:8 encourages believers to focus on what is virtuous and praiseworthy: "Finally, brethren, whatsoever things are true, whatsoever things are honest, whatsoever things are just, whatsoever things are pure, whatsoever things are lovely, whatsoever things are of good report; if there be any virtue, and if there be any praise, think on these things." This verse highlights the importance of directing one's thoughts toward what is true, noble, proper, pure, lovely, and admirable, reflecting a mindset on God's standards.

Living a holy life also involves guarding one's speech and actions. Ephesians 4:29 instructs, "Let no corrupt communication proceed out of your mouth, but that which is good to the use of edifying, that it may minister grace unto the hearers." This verse emphasizes the importance of speaking in a way that builds others up and imparts grace, avoiding corrupt or harmful language. Similarly, Colossians 3:17 advises, "And whatsoever ye do in word or deed, do all in the name of the Lord Jesus, giving thanks to God and the Father by him." This verse encourages believers to ensure that all their words and actions are done in the name of Jesus, reflecting gratitude and honor toward God.

Pursuing holiness also involves a commitment to ethical behavior and social justice. Micah 6:8 declares, "He hath shewed thee, O man, what is good; and what doth the LORD require of thee, but to do justly, and to love mercy, and to walk humbly with thy God?" This Old Testament verse emphasizes that God requires His people to act justly, love mercy, and walk humbly with Him, highlighting the ethical dimensions of holiness. The New Testament echoes these principles, calling believers to love their neighbors and seek justice and mercy.

Holiness and righteous living are also characterized by humility and repentance. James 4:8-10 exhorts, "Draw nigh to God, and he will draw nigh to you. Cleanse your hands, ye sinners; and purify your hearts, ye double minded. Be afflicted, and mourn, and weep: let your laughter be turned to mourning, and your joy to heaviness. Humble yourselves in the sight of the Lord, and he shall lift you up." This passage emphasizes the need for believers to draw near to God, cleanse themselves from sin, and humble themselves before Him, trusting that He will exalt them in due time.

Pursuing holiness also involves resisting the devil and standing firm in faith. 1 Peter 5:8-9 warns, "Be sober, be vigilant; because your adversary the devil, as a roaring lion, walketh about, seeking whom he may devour: Whom resist stedfast in the faith, knowing that the same afflictions are accomplished in your brethren that are in the world." This passage highlights the importance of vigilance and resistance against the devil, standing firm in faith despite the trials and temptations believers may face.

Living a holy life also means being a light to the world. Matthew 5:14-16 teaches, "Ye are the light of the world. A city that is set on an hill cannot be hid. Neither do men light a candle, and put it under a bushel, but on a candlestick; and it giveth light unto all that are in the house. Let your light so shine before men, that they may see your good works, and glorify your Father which is in heaven." This passage emphasizes that believers are called to be visible witnesses of God's light, reflecting His goodness through their actions and drawing others to glorify God.

The fruit of the Spirit, as described in Galatians 5:22-23, is another crucial aspect of holy and righteous living. These verses state, "But the fruit of the Spirit is love, joy, peace, longsuffering, gentleness, goodness, faith, Meekness, temperance: against such there is no law." This passage highlights the characteristics that should be evident in a believer living by the Spirit, reflecting God's character and holiness. The call to holiness also involves a commitment to spiritual growth and maturity. 2 Peter 3:18 encourages believers, "But grow in grace, and in the knowledge of our Lord and Saviour Jesus Christ. To him be glory both now and for ever. Amen." This verse emphasizes the importance of continual growth in grace and knowledge, striving to become more like Christ, and deepening one's relationship with Him.

Furthermore, holiness and righteous living are characterized by loving God and others. Matthew 22:37-39 records Jesus' teaching on the greatest commandments: "Jesus said unto him, Thou shalt love the Lord thy God with all thy heart, and with all thy soul, and with all thy mind. This is the first and great commandment. And the second is like unto it, Thou shalt love thy neighbour as thyself." These commandments highlight that true holiness involves loving God with all one's being and loving others as oneself, reflecting God's love in all relationships and interactions.

The pursuit of holiness also requires self-discipline and perseverance. Hebrews 12:1-2 exhorts, "Wherefore seeing we also are compassed about with so great a cloud of witnesses, let us lay aside every weight, and the sin which doth so easily beset us, and let us run with patience the race that is set before us, Looking unto Jesus the author and finisher of our faith; who for the joy that was set before him endured the cross, despising the shame, and is set down at the right hand of the throne of God." This passage encourages believers to lay aside all hindrances and sin, running the race of faith with perseverance and keeping their focus on Jesus.

Holiness and righteous living also involve practicing forgiveness and reconciliation. Matthew 6:14-15 teaches, "For if ye forgive men their trespasses, your heavenly Father will also forgive you: But if ye forgive not men their trespasses, neither will your Father forgive your trespasses." This passage emphasizes the importance of forgiving others as an essential aspect of living a holy life, recognizing that forgiveness reflects God's grace and mercy.

In summary, authentic Christianity, the heart of old-time religion, emphasizes holiness and righteous living, calling for holiness and separation from the world's sinful influences. 1 Peter 1:15-16 calls believers holy in all conversation, reflecting God's purity and righteousness. This involves resisting conformity to the world, pursuing righteousness, and being transformed by renewing the mind. Holiness is rooted in God's holy nature and involves sanctification, moral purity, integrity, and godly conduct. It requires guarding speech and actions, acting justly, loving mercy, and walking humbly with God. The pursuit of holiness includes humility, repentance, vigilance against the devil, and being a light to the world. The fruit of the Spirit, spiritual growth,

love for God and others, self-discipline, perseverance, forgiveness, and reconciliation are all essential aspects of holy and righteous living. By striving to live in a way that reflects God's holiness, believers fulfill their calling and glorify God in every aspect of their lives. This emphasis on holiness and righteous living is central to the message and mission of authentic Christianity, the heart of old-time religion.

Chapter 11 - Devoted To The Local Church

Authentic Christianity, the heart of old-time religion, strongly emphasizes the local church, which is essential for spiritual growth and encouragement. Fellowship with other believers is a vital aspect of the Christian faith, as highlighted in Hebrews 10:25, which says, "Not forsaking the assembling of ourselves together, as the manner of some is; but exhorting one another: and so much the more, as ye see the day approaching." This verse underscores the importance of gathering together for worship, study, and mutual support, emphasizing that as the return of Christ draws nearer, believers should be even more committed to meeting and encouraging one another.

The early church exemplifies the importance of the local church. Acts 2:42 describes the early Christians, "And they continued stedfastly in the apostles' doctrine and fellowship, and in breaking of bread, and in prayers." This passage shows that the early believers devoted themselves to the apostles' teaching, fellowship, the breaking of bread, and prayer. These activities were central to their local church and spiritual growth, reflecting a deep commitment to being together and supporting one another.

The local church provides opportunities for believers to encourage and build one another up. 1 Thessalonians 5:11 encourages, "Wherefore comfort yourselves together, and edify one another, even as also ye do." This verse highlights the importance of comforting and edifying one another, showing that mutual support and encouragement are vital components of Christian fellowship. Believers can offer and receive the encouragement needed to persevere in their faith by being part of a local church.

The fellowship also involves bearing one another's burdens. Galatians 6:2 instructs, "Bear ye one another's burdens, and so fulfil the law of Christ." This verse teaches that part of being in a local church is helping to carry the burdens of others, reflecting the love and care that Jesus showed. Bearing one another's burdens creates a strong sense of unity and support, helping believers navigate life's challenges together.

Gathering together for worship is a central aspect of the local church. Psalm 95:1-2 invites believers, "O come, let us sing unto the LORD: let us make a joyful noise to the rock of our salvation. Let us come before his presence with thanksgiving, and make a joyful noise unto him with psalms." This passage highlights the joy and importance of collectively coming together to worship God, expressing gratitude and praise. Worshiping together strengthens the local church and fosters a deeper connection with God.

The communal aspect of breaking bread or sharing meals is also significant in Christian fellowship. Acts 2:46 describes the early believers, "And they, continuing daily with one accord in the temple, and breaking bread from house to house, did eat their meat with gladness and singleness of heart." Sharing meals creates opportunities for deeper relationships and mutual care, reflecting the unity and joy of the early Christian community.

Prayer is another crucial element of fellowship. Matthew 18:20 says, "For where two or three are gathered together in my name, there am I in the midst of them." This verse emphasizes the presence of Jesus when believers gather to pray, showing the power and importance of the local church's prayers. Praying together strengthens the bonds between believers and invites God's presence and intervention in their lives.

Fellowship also includes studying the Bible together. 2 Timothy 3:16-17 affirms, "All scripture is given by inspiration of God, and is profitable for doctrine, for reproof, for correction, for instruction in righteousness: That the man of God may be perfect, thoroughly furnished unto all good works." Studying the Bible at a local church helps believers to grow in their understanding of God's Word, providing guidance and encouragement for living out their faith. Through collective study, believers can learn from one another and apply biblical principles.

The New Testament epistles frequently emphasize the importance of love and unity within the local church. John 13:34-35 records Jesus' command, "A new commandment I give unto you, That ye love one another; as I have loved you, that ye also love one another. By this shall all men know that ye are my disciples, if ye have love one to another." Love for one another is the defining mark of a true local church, demonstrating to the world the reality of Jesus' teachings and the Gospel's transformative power.

Forgiveness and reconciliation are also vital aspects of the local church. Colossians 3:13 instructs, "Forbearing one another, and forgiving one another, if any man have a quarrel against any: even as Christ forgave you, so also do ye." This verse emphasizes the importance of forgiving one another, reflecting the forgiveness that Christ has extended to us. Maintaining a spirit of forgiveness and reconciliation helps to preserve unity and peace within the local church.

Serving one another is another essential element of Christian fellowship. 1 Peter 4:10 encourages, "As every man hath received the gift, even so minister the same one to another, as good stewards of the manifold grace of God." This verse teaches that each believer has received gifts from God, which should be used to serve others within the local church. Serving one another fosters a spirit of humility and mutual support, strengthening the bonds of fellowship.

The local church also highlights hospitality as an essential practice. Romans 12:13 instructs, "Distributing to the necessity of saints; given to hospitality." This verse emphasizes the importance of being hospitable and opening one's home and resources to meet the needs of fellow believers. Hospitality creates opportunities for deeper relationships and demonstrates the love and care that characterize the local church.

Encouraging one another to live out their faith is another critical aspect of fellowship. Hebrews 3:13 advises, "But exhort one another daily, while it is called To day; lest any of you be hardened through the deceitfulness of sin." This verse highlights the importance of daily encouragement to help one another stay faithful and avoid the pitfalls of sin. Regular exhortation and encouragement within the community help believers to remain steadfast in their faith.

The early church provides a powerful example of the impact of the local church and fellowship. Acts 4:32 describes the unity and generosity of the early believers, "And the multitude of them that believed were of one heart and of one soul: neither said any of them that ought of the things which he possessed was his own; but they had all things common." This passage highlights the deep sense of unity and shared purpose that characterized the early church, demonstrating the transformative power of the Holy Spirit in bringing believers together.

The fellowship also involves mutual accountability and support. Proverbs 27:17 states, "Iron sharpeneth iron; so a man sharpeneth the countenance of his friend." This verse illustrates that believers help one another grow and improve through mutual accountability and support. Being part of a local church allows believers to challenge and encourage each other to live according to God's standards.

Corporate worship and fellowship also provide opportunities for communal expressions of faith. Ephesians 5:19 encourages, "Speaking to yourselves in psalms and hymns and spiritual songs, singing and making melody in your heart to the Lord." This verse highlights the joy and importance of singing and worshiping together, creating a sense of unity and shared worship within the local church.

The concept of the church as the body of Christ emphasizes the interconnectedness of believers. 1 Corinthians 12:12-14 explains, "For as the body is one, and hath many members, and all the members of that one body, being many, are one body: so also is Christ. For by one Spirit are we all baptized into one body, whether we be Jews or Gentiles, whether we be bond or free; and have been all made to drink into one Spirit. For the body is not one member, but many." This passage teaches that believers are part of one body, each with different roles and functions, but all essential to the health and functioning of the whole. This interconnectedness fosters a sense of belonging and mutual dependence within the local church.

Fellowship with other believers also strengthens individual faith and resilience. Ecclesiastes 4:9-12 illustrates the strength found in unity: "Two are better than one; because they have a good reward for their labour. For if they fall, the one will lift up his fellow: but woe to him that is alone when he falleth; for he hath not another to help him up. Again, if two lie together, then they have heat: but how can one be warm alone? And if one prevail against him, two shall withstand him; and a threefold cord is not quickly broken." This passage highlights the benefits of companionship and mutual support, showing that believers are stronger together than alone.

The New Testament also emphasizes the importance of being part of a local church. Acts 20:28 instructs church leaders, "Take heed therefore unto yourselves, and to all the flock, over the which the Holy Ghost hath made you overseers, to feed the church of God, which he hath purchased with his own blood." This verse underscores the responsibility of church leaders to care for and nurture the local congregation, recognizing the value and importance of each member.

Fellowship and community also play a role in discipleship and spiritual growth. 2 Timothy 2:2 advises, "And the things that thou hast heard of me among many witnesses, the same commit thou to faithful men, who shall be able to teach others also." This verse emphasizes the importance of passing on the teachings of the faith to others, creating a cycle of discipleship and growth within the local church.

In summary, authentic Christianity, the heart of old-time religion, strongly emphasizes the local church, which is essential for spiritual growth and encouragement. Hebrews 10:25 encourages believers not to forsake assembling but to exhort one another, especially as the day of Christ's return approaches. The early church exemplified the importance of community and fellowship through their devotion to teaching, fellowship, breaking bread, and prayer. The local church provides opportunities for encouragement, support, bearing one another's burdens, worship, sharing meals, and collective prayer. Studying the Bible together, practicing love and unity, forgiveness and reconciliation, serving one another, and showing hospitality are all vital aspects of Christian fellowship. The early church's unity and generosity, mutual accountability, corporate worship, and understanding of the church as the body of Christ highlight the interconnectedness and strength found in the local church. Being part of a local church, engaging in discipleship, and fostering spiritual growth are crucial components of authentic Christianity. Through the local church, believers can support and encourage one another, growing together in their faith and reflecting the love and unity that Jesus taught. This emphasis on the local church is central to the message and mission of authentic Christianity, the heart of old-time religion.

Chapter 12 - Durable Hope in Christ's Return

Authentic Christianity, the heart of old-time religion, strongly focuses on the steadfast hope in Christ's return, a central tenet of the faith. This belief in the anticipated return of Jesus Christ is not just a distant theological concept but a motivating force that shapes the lives and actions of believers. Titus 2:13 expresses this hope clearly, "Looking for that blessed hope, and the glorious appearing of the great God and our Saviour Jesus Christ." This verse emphasizes the importance of anticipating the return of Christ, described as a "blessed hope" and a "glorious appearing." This anticipation inspires believers to live faithfully and to share the Gospel with a sense of urgency, knowing that Christ could return at any moment.

The hope in Christ's return is a source of great encouragement and strength for believers. 1 Thessalonians 4:16-17 provides a vivid description of this event: "For the Lord himself shall descend from heaven with a shout, with the voice of the archangel, and with the trump of God: and the dead in Christ shall rise first: Then we which are alive and remain shall be caught up together with them in the clouds, to meet the Lord in the air: and so shall we ever be with the Lord." This passage assures believers that those who have died in Him will be resurrected at Christ's return, and those alive will be caught up with them to meet the Lord. The promise of being with the Lord forever is a source of immense hope and joy.

This anticipation of Christ's return encourages believers to live holy and godly lives. 2 Peter 3:11-12 urges, "Seeing then that all these things shall be dissolved, what manner of persons ought ye to be in all holy conversation and godliness, Looking for and hasting unto the coming of the day of God." This passage reminds believers that since the world will pass, they should focus on living holy and godly, preparing themselves for Christ's return. This focus on holiness and godliness aligns with the teachings of old-time religion, which emphasizes living in a way that honors God.

The certainty of Christ's return also motivates believers to remain steadfast in their faith. 1 Corinthians 15:58 encourages, "Therefore, my beloved brethren, be ye stedfast, unmoveable, always abounding in the work of the Lord, forasmuch as ye know that your labour is not in vain in the Lord." This verse calls believers to be steadfast and unmovable, always excelling in the work of the Lord, because they know that their efforts are not in vain. The hope of Christ's return provides a firm foundation for enduring faith and diligent service.

Believers are urged to be watchful and prepared for Christ's return. Matthew 24:42-44 warns, "Watch therefore: for ye know not what hour your Lord doth come. But know this, that if the goodman of the house had known in what watch the thief would come, he would have watched, and would not have suffered his house to be broken up. Therefore be ye also ready: for in such an hour as ye think not the Son of man cometh." This passage emphasizes the importance of being watchful and ready, as the exact timing of Christ's return is unknown. Believers are to live in a state of readiness, maintaining a close relationship with God and living according to His will.

The parable of the ten virgins in Matthew 25:1-13 further illustrates the need for readiness. The parable tells of ten virgins who took their lamps and went out to meet the bridegroom. Five were wise and brought extra oil, while five were foolish and did not. When the bridegroom came, the wise virgins were ready and went in with him to the wedding banquet, but the foolish virgins were shut out. Jesus concludes the parable with the warning, "Watch therefore, for ye know neither the day nor the hour wherein the Son of man cometh." This parable highlights the importance of being prepared and vigilant, living in a way ready for Christ's return at any moment.

The hope of Christ's return inspires believers to share the Gospel urgently. Matthew 28:19-20, known as the Great Commission, commands, "Go ye therefore, and teach all nations, baptizing them in the name of the Father, and of the Son, and of the Holy Ghost: Teaching them to observe all things whatsoever I have commanded you: and, lo, I am with you alway, even unto the end of the world." The anticipation of Christ's return fuels the urgency to spread the Gospel to all nations, making disciples and teaching them to observe Christ's commandments. This mission is driven by the understanding that time is short and the need for salvation is great.

The New Testament frequently emphasizes the imminence of Christ's return. James 5:8-9 states, "Be ye also patient; stablish your hearts: for the coming of the Lord draweth nigh. Grudge not one against another, brethren, lest ye be condemned: behold, the judge standeth before the door." This passage encourages believers to be patient and to strengthen their hearts, knowing that the Lord's coming is near. It also warns against grumbling against one another, reminding believers that Christ, the judge, is at the door.

The anticipation of Christ's return also provides comfort in times of suffering and persecution. Romans 8:18 offers hope, "For I reckon that the sufferings of this present time are not worthy to be compared with the glory which shall be revealed in us." This verse reassures believers that the present sufferings are temporary and insignificant compared to the eternal glory that will be revealed when Christ returns. This perspective helps believers to endure hardships with hope and patience.

The Apostle Paul frequently spoke of the hope of Christ's return. In Philippians 3:20-21, he writes, "For our conversation is in heaven; from whence also we look for the Saviour, the Lord Jesus Christ: Who shall change our vile body, that it may be fashioned like unto his glorious body, according to the working whereby he is able even to subdue all things unto himself." This passage emphasizes that believers' faithful citizenship is in heaven, and they eagerly await the return of Jesus Christ, who will transform their mortal bodies to be like His glorious body.

This hope of transformation and eternal life motivates believers to live faithfully.

The return of Christ is also a key theme in Revelation. Revelation 22:12-13 records Jesus' promise, "And, behold, I come quickly; and my reward is with me, to give every man according as his work shall be. I am Alpha and Omega, the beginning and the end, the first and the last." This promise assures believers that Jesus will return soon, bringing rewards according to each person's deeds. The anticipation of this reward encourages believers to persevere in their faith and good works.

Believers are called to encourage one another with the hope of Christ's return. 1 Thessalonians 4:18 advises, "Wherefore comfort one another with these words." This verse follows Paul's detailed description of the resurrection and the rapture, urging believers to comfort and encourage each other with the promise of Christ's return. This mutual encouragement strengthens God's children and helps believers remain hopeful and steadfast.

The hope of Christ's return also influences how believers view their possessions and priorities. Colossians 3:2-4 instructs, "Set your affection on things above, not on things on the earth. For ye are dead, and your life is hid with Christ in God. When Christ, who is our life, shall appear, then shall ye also appear with him in glory." This passage encourages believers to focus on heavenly things rather than earthly possessions, recognizing that their true life is hidden with Christ and will be fully revealed when He returns.

The anticipation of Christ's return also calls for ethical and moral living. 1 John 3:2-3 states, "Beloved, now are we the sons of God, and it doth not yet appear what we shall be: but we know that, when he shall appear, we shall be like him; for we shall see him as he is. And every man that hath this hope in him purifieth himself, even as he is pure." This passage emphasizes that the hope of being like Christ when He returns motivates believers to purify themselves and live in a way that reflects His purity.

The hope of Christ's return also encourages believers to remain vigilant and spiritually awake. Romans 13:11-12 advises, "And that, knowing the time, that now it is high time to awake out of sleep: for now is our salvation nearer than when we believed. The night is far spent, the day is at hand: let us therefore cast off the works of darkness, and let us put on the armour of light." This passage urges believers to wake up from spiritual complacency, recognize that the return of Christ is closer than ever, and live in the light of this reality.

The anticipation of Christ's return is a powerful motivator for a life of faithfulness and devotion. Hebrews 9:28 promises, "So Christ was once offered to bear the sins of many; and unto them that look for him shall he appear the second time without sin unto salvation." This verse reassures believers that Christ, who offered Himself to bear the sins of many, will appear a second time to bring salvation to those who eagerly await Him. This promise fuels the hope and expectation of believers, encouraging them to remain faithful and vigilant.

In conclusion, authentic Christianity, the heart of old-time religion, strongly focuses on the steadfast hope in Christ's return. Titus 2:13 expresses this hope, calling it "that blessed hope, and the glorious appearing of the great God and our Saviour Jesus Christ." The anticipation of Christ's return shapes the lives and actions of believers, motivating them to live faithfully and share the Gospel with urgency. This hope provides encouragement and strength, inspires holiness and godliness, and encourages believers to remain steadfast in their faith. It calls for watchfulness and readiness, promotes mutual encouragement, and influences priorities and ethical living. The return of Christ is a central theme throughout the New Testament, providing comfort in times of suffering and persecution and promising transformation and eternal life. The anticipation of Christ's return is a powerful motivator for living a life of faithfulness and devotion, shaping the character and actions of believers as they await the fulfillment of God's promises. This emphasis on the hope of Christ's return is central to the message and mission of authentic Christianity, the heart of old-time religion.

Don't miss out!

Visit the website below and you can sign up to receive emails whenever Joshua Rhoades publishes a new book. There's no charge and no obligation.

https://books2read.com/r/B-A-AJLBB-TDKUE

BOOKS 2 READ

Connecting independent readers to independent writers.

Did you love *Authentic Christianity: The Heart of Old Time Religion*? Then you should read *Courage Under Fire: David's Stand On The Battlefield*[1] by Joshua Rhoades!

[2]

Courage Under Fire: David's Stand on the Battlefield" recounts the stirring first-person narrative of David, a young shepherd boy who faced the colossal Philistine warrior, Goliath, armed with nothing but a sling, a few stones, and an unwavering faith in God. My journey begins with my humble obedience to my father, Jesse, who sent me to deliver provisions to my brothers on the front lines. Despite their scoffing and jeers at my presence on the battlefield, I remained undeterred, feeling a deep sense of duty not only to my family but also to the cause they were fighting for. This sense of duty brought me before King Saul, who, upon hearing my bold offer to fight Goliath, expressed severe doubts about my abilities.

---

1. https://books2read.com/u/3G7wPP

2. https://books2read.com/u/3G7wPP

He looked upon my youthful frame and could not see how I, with no armor or sword, could face such a fearsome giant.Goliath himself, towering and menacing, mocked me as I stepped onto the battlefield, his words heavy with contempt and surety of victory. His towering figure clad in armor, with a spear like a weaver's beam, seemed invincible. Yet, as he taunted me, I felt a profound calm settle over me; I knew that the battle was not mine but the Lord's. I declared as much to Goliath, telling him that the God of the armies of Israel whom he had defied would deliver him into my hands. With a simple sling and a stone, and faith as my greatest weapon, I struck the Philistine on his forehead. The giant fell face down to the ground, and I stood over him, a boy no longer underestimated but recognized as the instrument through which God showed His power.This historical moment is not merely a testament to my personal courage but serves as a beacon of inspiration for every Christian facing their own "Goliaths." Whether these giants are doubts, fears, or seemingly insurmountable challenges, the story exemplifies how faith in God equips us to overcome them. The practical lessons derived from this experience emphasize the importance of obedience, humility, and trust in God's power over our own. In moments of trial, we, like I once did, can draw strength from understanding that God's purposes will prevail over our adversities. As I recount my stand on the battlefield, it becomes clear that true victory in life comes from putting our faith into action, trusting in the Lord's guidance, and stepping forward with courage, even when the odds seem overwhelmingly against us.

www.ingramcontent.com/pod-product-compliance
Lightning Source LLC
Chambersburg PA
CBHW061401160726

47995CB00001B/418